First Experiences

Danny goes to the Dentist

Written by **Robert Robinson**
Illustrated by **Nicola Smee**

BRIMAX

It's almost time for bed. Mother is reading Danny and Vicki a book about looking after your teeth. Tomorrow they are going to visit the dentist.

The dentist is not far from where they live.
Danny and Vicki run down the path to the
dentist's surgery.

"The children have come for a check up," says Mother, and tells the receptionist their names. The receptionist finds Danny and Vicki's records.

The waiting room is full of people. Danny sees his friend, Matthew. The boys play together while they wait. Mother reads Vicki a story.

Soon the nurse comes to lead the way to the dentist's room. Mother goes with Danny and Vicki.

"Hello, you two," says the dentist. "How are you?"
"I've lost my first baby tooth," says Danny, proudly.
"You'll lose more as you get older," replies the
dentist, "and get new ones in their place."

"Now then, who wants to be first?" he asks.
"Me please," says Vicki, climbing on to the chair.

The nurse ties a special bib around Vicki's neck to stop her clothes from getting wet.

"I like this chair," says Vicki. "Can you make it go up and down like you did last time?"
"Of course," laughs the dentist.
Vicki points to the button that adjusts the chair.

"Open your mouth wide," says the dentist. He gently checks Vicki's teeth with a thin, pointed instrument. He uses a little mirror on a stick to see the top ones.

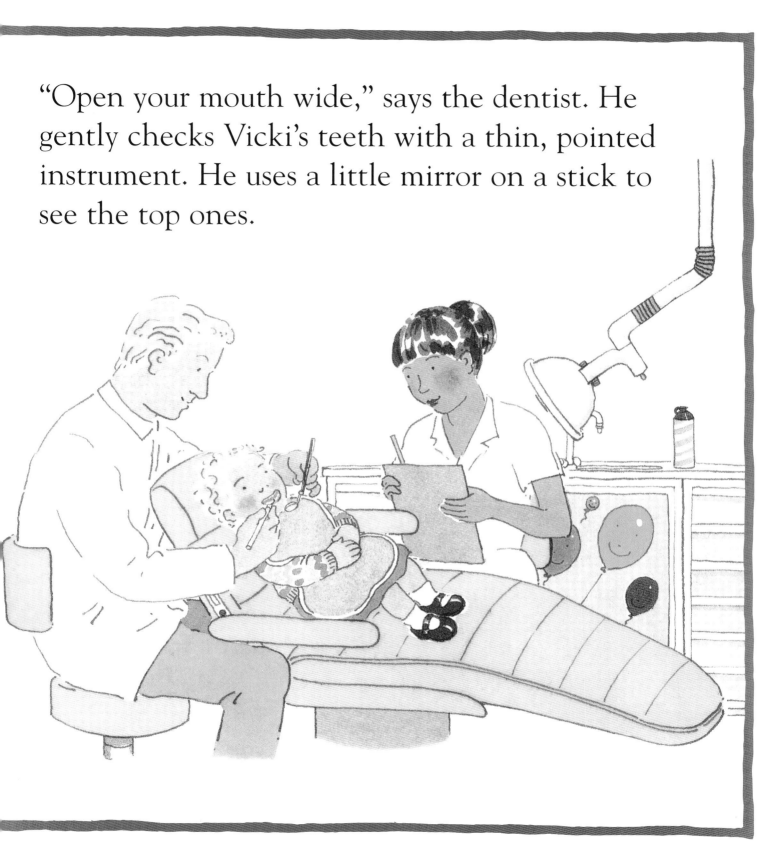

Mother and Danny wait while the dentist checks Vicki's teeth.

"Your teeth seem fine, Vicki," says the dentist. "Now I'll give them a polish to make them extra clean." Vicki likes having her teeth polished. The brush tickles and the paste has a minty taste.

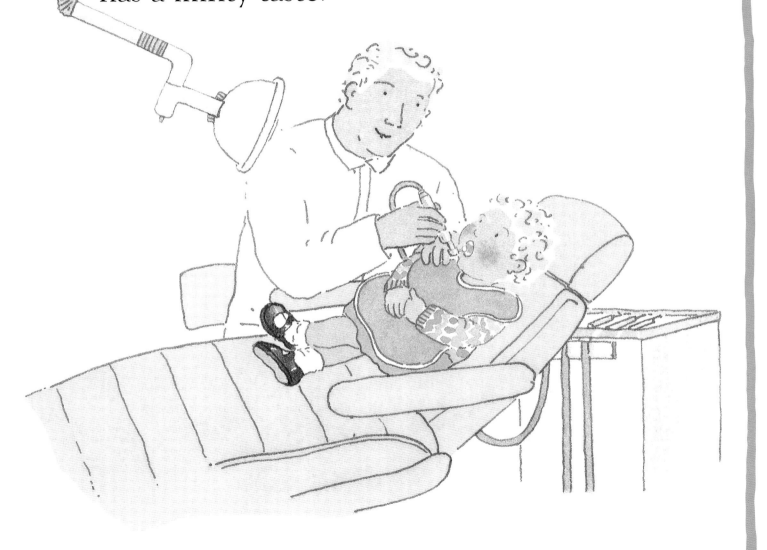

"Your turn now, Danny," says the dentist. "I want to see if your new tooth is coming through." Danny sits on the chair and opens his mouth wide.

The dentist looks at Danny's teeth and tells the nurse what he sees. The nurse makes notes on Danny's record. "Don't forget about his new tooth," says Vicki.

The dentist finds a hole in one of Danny's teeth. "I think you have been eating too many sweet things," he says.

"I am going to clean the hole with my drill and put a filling in the tooth." The drill makes a whining noise, but it doesn't hurt.

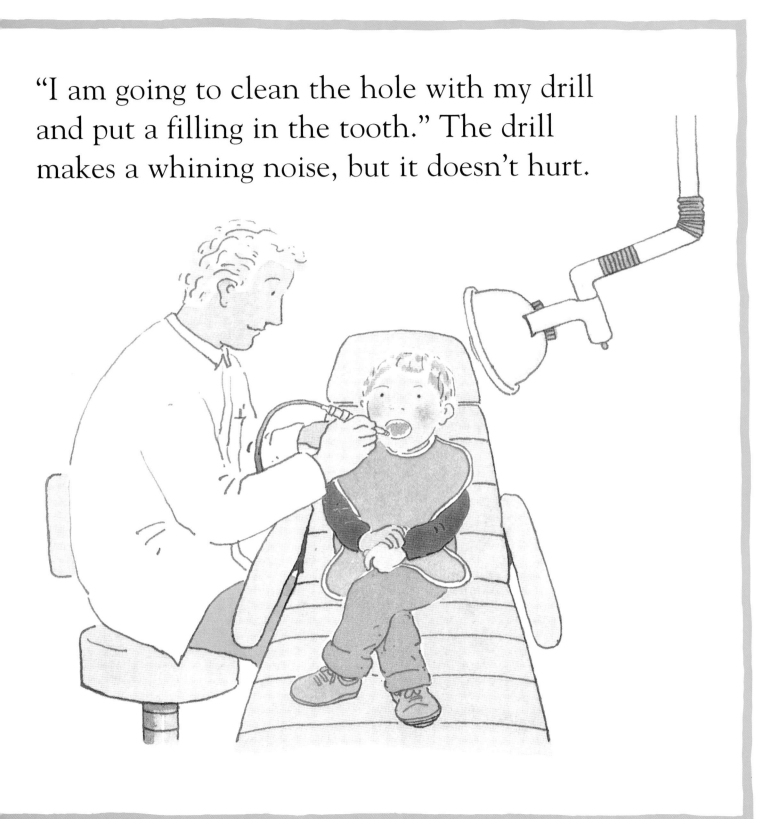

The nurse makes a filling mixture that looks like white toothpaste. The dentist fills Danny's tooth with it. "Leave your mouth open for a minute while the mixture hardens," he says.

When the filling has set, Danny takes a sip of mouthwash. He swishes it around his mouth and spits into a funnel.

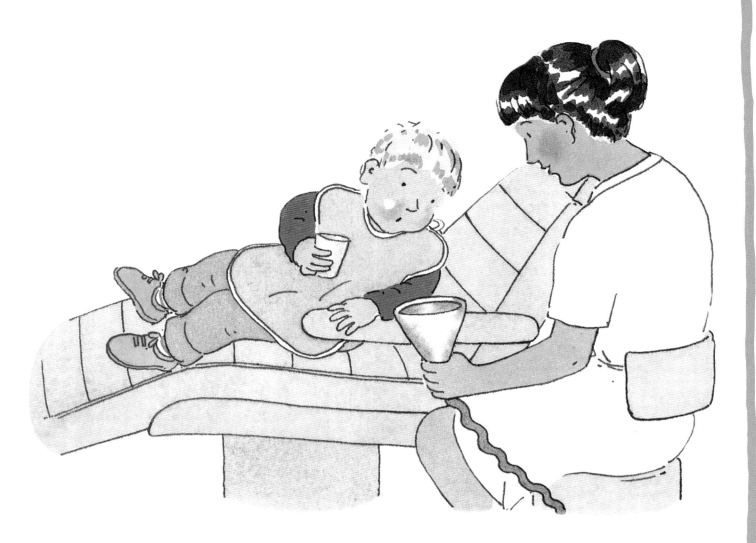

"All done," says the dentist. "Now remember to take good care of your teeth. I want you to brush them twice a day and try not to eat too many sweets." He gives Danny and Vicki balloons and a poster.

On the way out, the receptionist lets Danny and Vicki choose a sticker. Mother buys the children a new toothbrush each.

At bedtime, Danny and Vicki use their new toothbrushes. They clean their teeth really well and remove every bit of food.

Mother puts up the poster in their room. "If I eat what the poster tells me, I hope I won't need another filling," says Danny.

Eat these
for treats
NOT
sticky sweets.